PUPPY LOVE

The Story of Esme and Sam

For my dear New York friends—Simone, Dominic, Max, and Jack Ciafardini—G. S.

For my darling children, Esme and Sam—E. H.

SIMON & SCHUSTER BOOKS FOR YOUNG READERS
An imprint of Simon & Schuster Children's Publishing Division
1230 Avenue of the Americas, New York, New York 10020
Text copyright © 2008 by Gillian Shields
Illustrations copyright © 2008 by Elizabeth Harbour
First published in Great Britain in 2008 by Simon & Schuster UK Ltd
First U.S. edition 2009
SIMON & SCHUSTER BOOKS FOR YOUNG READERS is a trademark of Simon & Schuster, Inc.
The text for this book is set in Baskerville.
Manufactured in China
2 4 6 8 10 9 7 5 3 1
Library of Congress Cataloging-in-Publication Data
Shields, Gillian.
Puppy love : the story of Esme and Sam / Gillian Shields ; illustrated
by Elizabeth Harbour.
p. cm.
ISBN: 978-1-4169-8010-0 (hardcover : alk. paper)
1. Puppies—Juvenile poetry. 2. Dogs—Juvenile poetry. 3. Children's
poetry, American. I. Harbour, Elizabeth, ill. II. Title.
PS3619.H537P87 2009
811'.6—dc22
2008041869

PUPPY LOVE
The Story of Esme and Sam

Gillian Shields & Elizabeth Harbour

SIMON & SCHUSTER BOOKS FOR YOUNG READERS

New York   London   Toronto   Sydney

This is the city and this is the park,
Where dogs run and play with a yap and a bark.

Here is the dog called Esme Lamour,
Who lives in a penthouse on the top floor.

And here is the dog called Samuel Bloom,
Who lives in a crowded tenement room.

Esme lunches on chicken and crab,
Samuel eats any scraps he can grab.

Esme relaxes on satins and lace,
Samuel sleeps wherever there's space.

Promptly at three Esme walks in the park,

Where Samuel prowls alone when it's dark.

One afternoon, all sunny and bright,

Mrs. B. Goldstein had such a bad fright:

Esme's pink leash somehow slipped from her collar,
And Mrs. B. Goldstein started to holler.
But Esme was after some freedom and fun,
So she followed her nose and started to run.

It was all so exciting, so thrilling and new,
Until the day faded and long shadows grew.
Esme ran to the left, Mrs. B. to the right!
And quickly, too quickly, the day turned to night.

Mrs. B. Goldstein went sadly back home,
And called the police on her gold telephone;
"Oh, do find my darling! She's lost and it's dark!
Send all of your men to search through the park!"

Poor little Esme was starting to shiver,
Alone and afraid, her heart all a-quiver.

Esme was frightened of all she could see,
A horse like a ghost, and a rat, and a tree.
But . . .

Samuel Bloom was coming uptown,

To walk in the park, since the sun had gone down.

Samuel Bloom was the king of the night!

Samuel Bloom could make it all right.

Under a bush, just by the lake,

He found Esme Lamour in a terrible quake.

"Hey kid, what's the problem?" he said. "Don't be down.

You're in the Big Apple—it's my kinda town!"

"But I'm lost," she replied, with a soft, timid smile.

"Follow me." Samuel grinned. "It's less than a mile!"

So he led, and she followed, by lake and by zoo . . .

By grottoes and arbors, where wild roses grew.

They walked and they talked, and a sweet night bird sang.
They talked and they walked, as the old church bell rang.

He showed her the stars and the great shining moon,
And in Esme's heart, love started to bloom.
"Oh, darling," she gasped, "can this really be true?"
And that's when he said, "It's true—I love you!"

When dawn came, by Esme's splendid front door,
They pledged their true love, forever, and more.

But old Mrs. B. didn't see it that way,
She grabbed hold of Esme and chased Sam away.
"Has that nasty, rough doggy been horrid, my dear?
We'll make sure he never comes hanging round here."

So Samuel slipped back to his tenement's gloom,

Unlucky, unhappy, poor Samuel Bloom!

Esme was back with her satins and silk,

Her lobsters and steaks, her eggs and her milk.

But without Samuel Bloom, the world seemed so gray . . .

So Esme Lamour, one day, ran away!

Downtown she flew, with her heart in her mouth,
To reach her true love, she had to head south.

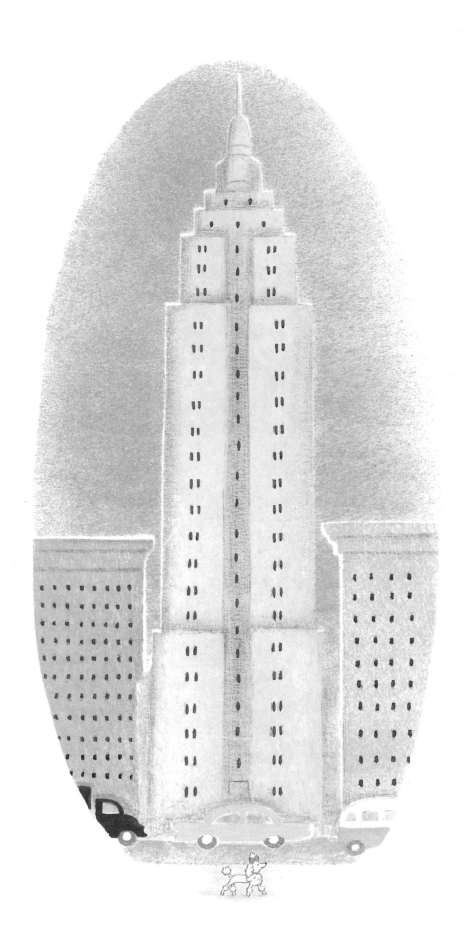

Past buildings so tall, down avenues long,

Her love made her brave, her love made her strong.

Past busy downtown streets, with long traffic jams . . .

Past China, past Italy, past cheeses and hams . . .

She raced up the steps to the tenement room,
And that's where she found her Samuel Bloom.
"Hey, kid!" exclaimed Sam. "Is that you at the door?"
"Yes, darling," she answered, "forever, and more."

Now this is the city and this is the park,

Where dogs run and play with a yap and a bark.

Promptly at three, rain or shine, every day,

Mrs. B. Goldstein comes walking this way.

And with her walk Esme, and Samuel Bloom,

Plus five little puppies, as round as the moon.

The End